For Pilar, who loves to
make up stories, too. — JB

To my parents, for teaching me
that dreams are worth chasing.
We may even get to live them. — KR

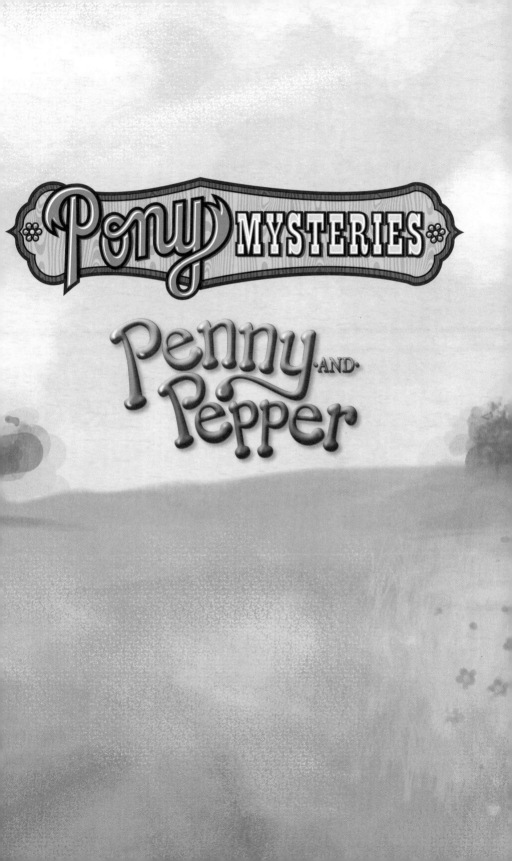

Pony MYSTERIES

Penny ·AND· Pepper

Library of Congress Cataloging-in-Publication Data
Betancourt, Jeanne.
 Pony mysteries : Penny and Pepper / by Jeanne Betancourt ; illustrated by Kellee Riley. -- 1st ed.
     p. cm. -- (Pony mysteries)
 Summary: Penny Ryder is happy to spend a summer in the country with her grandparents, but she is not sure about Pepper the pony or the neighbor twins until Pepper disappears and the twins, Tina and Tom, help find him.
 ISBN 978-0-545-11508-7 (pbk.)
 [1. Ponies--Fiction. 2. Lost and found possessions--Fiction. 3. Country life--Fiction. 4. Brothers and sisters--Fiction. 5. Twins--Fiction. 6. Mystery and detective stories.] I. Riley, Kellee, ill. II. Title. III. Series.

 PZ7.B46626Ppe 2011
 [E]--dc22

2010020585

ISBN 978-0-545-11508-7

10 9 8 7 6 5 4 3   11 12 13 14 15

Printed in the U.S.A.   40
First edition, January 2011

By Jeanne Betancourt

Illustrated by Kellee Riley

Cartwheel
·B·O·O·K·S·®

SCHOLASTIC INC.
New York   Toronto   London   Auckland
Sydney   Mexico City   New Delhi   Hong Kong

Table of Contents

Chapter 1
A BIG SURPRISE

My name is Penny Ryder.

I live in the city.

My whole family lives in the city.

But my grandparents live in the country.

Grandma and Grandpa want me to stay

with them for the whole summer.

So here I am.

"We have a big surprise for you," says
Grandma.

"Two big surprises," says Grandpa.

"THREE big surprises," says Grandma.

"Three surprises?" I say. I look around
the kitchen. "Where?"

I follow Grandma and Grandpa out the back door, down the porch steps, and into their big backyard.

A shaggy brown pony is standing under a tree.

"Is that my surprise?" I ask. "A pony?"

"Yes," answers Grandpa. "His name is Pepper."

Chapter 2
LAUGHING TWINS

The pony runs toward us. He is very fast.
I am afraid that he will knock me over.
He stops in front of me and sniffs my
purple bag.

"Do you have a snack in that bag, Miss
Penny?" asks Grandma.
"An apple," I answer.
"An apple is a perfect treat for your new
pet," says Grandpa.

I hold the apple out for Pepper.

Pepper grabs the apple with his slobbery mouth.

I step back and fall on my bottom.

I hear someone laughing.

I see two someones laughing.

A boy and girl are at the other end of the backyard.

Grandpa helps me up.

I try to brush the mud off my new pink swirly skirt.

Pepper turns. His tail swishes in my face.
He is running to the girl and boy.
The boy and girl are running to Pepper.
They are not afraid of slobbering ponies.

"Here are surprises number two and three,"
says Grandpa. "Tina and Tom Granger.
They are our neighbors."
"Tina and Tom are twins," says Grandma.
"They have been waiting to meet you."

Tom and Tina come to our house every day
to play in the backyard with Pepper.
I do not like the backyard.
I stay inside and draw with my sparkle
markers.
Sometimes I read. I like to read mysteries.

One day, Tina and Tom draw with me.
"You are lucky to have a pony," says Tom.
"I wish I had a pony."
I say, "I wish I had a cat. My cat would
have a pink collar with sparkles. That would
be so cute."

"But Pepper is so cute," says Tina. "Just look at him." She points out the kitchen window. We all look out the window, but we cannot see Pepper in the backyard.

"He's not there," Tom says.
"Where is he?" I say.
"Maybe he is in his shed," says Tina.
We run outside to look for Pepper.

Pepper is not in his shed.

He is not next to his shed.

He is not behind his shed.

He is not anywhere in that whole
big backyard.

Chapter 3
MISSING PONY

"Maybe he ran away," I say.

"He could be lost," says Tom.

"Or hurt," says Tina.

"How did he get out?" asks Tom.

"We have to be detectives," I say. "And solve the mystery."

"We have to look for clues," says Tina.

"Maybe Pepper jumped over the fence," says Tom.

We all look at the fence. It is very high. "I don't think Pepper can jump that high," says Tina.

"Maybe he went through the gate," I say. "The gate is locked," says Tom. "I locked it when we came here this morning."

I run over to the gate. It swings open.

"Pepper must have opened it with his mouth," says Tina.

"He is a smart pony," says Tom.

"He is a missing pony," I say. "But we have clue #1. The clue is: Pepper went through this gate."

We go through the gate and stand on a wide path.

"This is Town Trail," explains Tina. "It is a riding trail."

Tina points to the left. "That's the way to our goat farm," she says.

Tom points to the right. "That way goes deeper into the woods," he says.

I think the woods are scary.

I look down at my purple shoes with satin bows.

They are already covered in mud.

I want to go back to the house, but I have to find Pepper.

I smell something that makes me forget about my muddy shoes. Tom has smelled it, too.

Tom points to the trail going to the right.
There is a pile of fresh, smelly pony plop.
"There is clue #2," he says. "A pony went in
this direction."

We walk on Town Trail looking for more clues.

Tina spots a piece of shiny red ribbon with silver sparkles. The ribbon is caught on a tree branch. She holds it up for Tom and me to see.
"I put that ribbon in Pepper's mane this morning," she says.

"That ribbon is clue #3," I say. "The pony that came this way is Pepper."

"And here is clue #4," says Tina. She is pointing at hoofprints in a muddy section of the trail.

We run along the trail.

"Pepper can run a lot faster than we can," says Tina.

"He might go off the trail," says Tom.

"And get lost in the woods," I add.

We run faster.

We stop at a fork in the trail.
Which way did Pepper go?

"Look for more clues," I say.
"Shish," says Tina. "I hear something."

Chapter 4
A CLUE IN THE BUSH

We all listen. First we hear a rustling noise.
Next we hear a little neigh.
"Clue #5," I whisper.
We run left toward the sounds.

I am the first one to see Pepper.
Tina runs up to him and puts her arms
around his neck.
"Pepper," she says. "We were scared you
were lost."

Pepper doesn't pay any attention to Tina. He is too busy sniffing at a bush.

"What is he doing?" I ask.

"There is something in the bush that he wants," answers Tom.

I hear a meow.
It is a frightened meow.

I kneel down and look inside the bush. Two little green eyes look back at me.
"There's a kitten in there," I tell Tom and Tina. "It is caught inside."

Pepper neighs softly and nudges Tina toward the bush.

He wants us to help the kitten.

We move the branches and lift the kitten out.

"It's okay, kitty," I say softly. "We will take care of you."

The kitten is black with white on its neck and paws.

Pepper comes over to sniff the kitten. He is very gentle.

The kitten is not afraid of Pepper.

Pepper and the kitten rub noses.

We walk back to my house. The kitten snuggles in my arms and falls fast asleep.

"Pepper was not lost," says Tom. "He heard the kitten and went looking for her."

"He smelled her, too," I say. "Those were Pepper's clues. Pepper is a detective."

Chapter 5
DETECTIVES ON PARADE

We give Pepper an apple.

We give the cat some goat's milk.

Grandpa gives us cookies and juice.

The kitten explores the shed and yard.

Pepper follows her everywhere.

Tom, Tina, and I sit at the picnic table to have our snack.

"That kitten needs a name," says Tina.

"We should make a list of names," I say.

"And then vote."

There are five names on our list:

Fluffy
Lucky
Sparkles
Sweetie
Tuxedo

We each write down our favorite name on a little piece of paper and fold it.

I open the first paper.
The name on the paper is Lucky.
I open the second paper.
The name on the paper is Lucky.
I hold up my folded paper.
I know what it says.

I tell Tom and Tina, "I voted for Lucky, too."
"Lucky is a perfect name," we all say at the
same time.

I point to Pepper. "Look."
Pepper's head is bent toward Lucky.
Lucky walks up Pepper's head and onto
his back.
Pepper slowly lifts his head and Lucky
snuggles into his mane.

"Lucky is lucky that Pepper found her," says Tina. "Now she has a good home."

"Pepper and Lucky are lucky that they are friends," I say.

"And we're lucky that we are friends," says Tina.

"And good detectives," adds Tom.

"Yes," I agree, "we are all lucky."

Pepper gives Lucky a ride around the backyard.
We line up behind Pepper and march around the yard, too.

Pepper stops and turns to me. He twitches his ears and neighs softly.
I put my cheek against his.
"Pepper," I say, "you are the best."
Lucky meows. I look at her little face. "You too, Lucky," I say. "You are the best kitten."

We continue our parade around the yard.
A kitten and four detectives—Pepper, Tina,
Tom, and me, Penny Ryder.